Lorenzo Pignotti

Robert Manners

A Poem

Lorenzo Pignotti

Robert Manners
A Poem

ISBN/EAN: 9783744764575

Printed in Europe, USA, Canada, Australia, Japan

Cover: Foto ©Andreas Hilbeck / pixelio.de

More available books at **www.hansebooks.com**

ROBERT MANNERS

A POEM

TRANSLATED FROM THE ITALIAN

BY

A MEMBER OF THE ROYAL ACADEMY

OF FLORENCE

Dulce et decorum eſt pro Patria mori .
Horat.

FLORENCE MDCCLXXXV.

PRINTED FOR G. CAM. PRINTER TO HIS ROYAL HIGHNESS
WITH PERMISSION

CARLO
DUCA DI RUTLAND

CAV.^{RE} DEL NOBILISSIMO ORDINE

DELLA GIARRETTIERA &c. &c.

E

VICERÈ D' IRLANDA.

NOn vi maravigliate, o Signore, fe le Mufe Italiane ardifcono di alzar la voce fulle fponde del Tamigi. Voi fapete che il loro più caro oggetto fù fempre celebrare gl' Eroi, onde vengono volentieri a tro-

TO HIS GRACE

CHARLES

DUKE OF RUTLAND

K. G. &c. &c.

LORD LIEUTENANT

OF

THE KINGDOM OF IRELAND.

Let it not surprize your Grace that the Italian muses should dare to raise the song upon the banks of the Thames. You well know that their chief delight has ever been to celebrate Heroes, and that they offer

vargli ove fono. La Libertà gl' à fempre
prodotti, e l' Italia fi ricorda ancora quanto
n' è ftata feconda. E chi merita più quefto
nome del voftro illuftre fratello, il quale
benchè diftinto co i più rari favori dalla
fortuna, che aveva riunito in lui e le grazie
amabili della gioventù, e il rango il più ele-
vato, e le più ampie ricchezze, tuttavìa non
tenendo verun conto di sì fatti vantaggi,
credè di dover cercar la gloria folamente
colle proprie azioni, e corfe fubito per la
ftrada più atta a procacciargliela, cioè a fer-
vir la Patria, e facrificarfi per lei? Non v' è
quafi avvenimento memorabile nell' ultima
guerra, in cui non fiafi onorevolmente
diftinto, coronando poi le fue imprefe
con una morte illuftre nella battaglia del
dì 12 Aprile 1782 nella frefca età d' anni 24: morte immatura pel numero degl'
anni, ma non delle azioni. Quefte fon
tali, che il Poeta ha dovuto far da puro
iftorico. I colori poetici che adornando la

themselves most willingly where such Heroes may be found. Liberty is the parent
of true Heroism, of which Italy yet remem-
bers how fruitful she has been. And who
can be more deserving of the name of Hero,
than your Grace's noble Brother, who al-
though distinguished by every advantage of
youth and rank, which however he but little
prized, considered real glory to be alone
acquired by personal merit, and the actions
of the individual. He therefore took the shor-
test road to obtain it by serving his Country, and by sacrificing himself in her cause.
He was most honourably distinguished in
almost every event of the late war, and
crowned the whole by a glorious death at
the age of 24 years, and in the famous
battle of the memorable 12 of April 1782.
a death immature indeed in respect of years,
but far otherwise in point of greatness. The
Poet here endeavours to celebrate the
actions of the Hero with the exactness of the

verità talora quaſi la naſcondono, ſe ſi ſoffrono quando dipingono i faꞏti dell' età da noi diſtanti, non poſſono aver luogo innanzi ai contemporanei, e teſtimonj oculari; fortunatamente nel noſtro caſo la verità nuda è sì bella, che gl' ornamenti non farebbero che sfigurarla, e coprirne delle grazie.

Offro pertanto ad un fratello tanto illuſtre nelle arti di pace, e che ſerve in eſſe sì utilmente la Patria, l' iſtoria delle impreſe dell' altro fratello, che l' à sì ben ſervita col ſangue, e col più umile oſſequio ho l' onore di dirmi.

Umiliſſimo e Obbligatiſs. Servitore
Lorenzo Pignotti.

Historian ; for the poetic ornaments , which are excusable , and in fact necessary to set off the fame of those , who lived in times long past, must give offence to contemporaries , and eye witnesses . Fortunately in this instance , the plain truth is in itself so splendid , that all embellishment would appear a diminution .

I offer therefore to one Brother renowned in the arts of peace , and who renders himself truly useful to his Country, the history of the valiant enterprizes of the other, who has so well served that Country with' his blood , & with the most profound humility declare myself.

Your Grace's

Most obliged Humble Servant ,
Lorenzo Pignotti .

O Dea, non tu, che le lafcive chiome
Cinta di rofe, fra gl'aonj mirti
Giaci in languidi vezzi, e delle molli
Corde al tenero fuon guidi la danza:
Ma tu che fopra dirupata balza
Di Pindo, di furor facro atteggiata,
Fiammeggiante le gote, e nobilmente
Scompofta il crine in maeftà negletta
Siedi, e gl'erranti lumi, e l'agitate
Palme inalzando al Ciel, di fcuoter tenti
E fchiuder dall'angufte vie del labro
In forti carmi il Dio, che in petto volvi:
Tu che col fuon della guerriera tromba
Canti gl'Eroi che per la Patria il fangue
Intrepidi verfaro, ah fcendi, e in feno
Nel freddo fen vibrami un raggio amico
Di quella nobil fiamma, onde a fuoi figli
Il Nume il più benefico a i mortali
La Libertà rifcalda il core, e fopra

*T*hee I invoke not Goddeſs! Who with hair
In roſes bound, amidſt Aonian myrtle
At eaſe reclin'ſt, and as the languid harp
Breathes, ſweetly wild, the ſoul-ſubduing ſtrain,
Call'ſt the fond lovers to th'expreſſive dance.
But thee; who on the rugged frowning rock
Of Pindus ſit'ſt, in mournful act of woe,
And ſacred fury that inflames the breaſt:
With burning cheek, with copious locks that ſtray
In looſe diſorder, and neglected pride;
With wand'ring eyes, and arms outſtretcht to heaven,
While from the narrow paſſage of thy lips,
Thou ſtriv'ſt to pour in ſtrong, harmonious verſe,
The warm divinity that rules within.
Yes, thee I call, who with majeſtic ſound
Of ſolemn trump, th'intrepid heroes praiſe
Delight'ſt to ſing, heroes, who nobly ſhed
Their blood, to ſave their country, hither come,
And in my breaſt illume one glowing ſpark
Of the celeſtial flame, which liberty

Il ſuol gli leva, e rende eguali a i Numi.
Quel ſacro raggio allor che un alma accende
O da vigor per le ſublimi impreſe,
O per cantarle. O Dea quanto ſovente
Viſitaſti le a te dilette un giorno
Di virtù ſì feconde itale ſpiagge!
Rammenta quando le ſonanti penne
Sulla Rupe Tarpea, ſopra i latini
Colli ſpiegavi a rimirar con baſſa
Fronte i Re prigionieri, e in torvo volto
Il domito Germano il Parto altiero
Guerniti di barbarici ornamenti
Paſſare in ordin lungo, e dell' Eufrate
Del Ren del Tigri i ſimulacri meſti
Coll' urna rotta irti l' algoſo crine
Straſcinati nel fango a te davanti.
Tu ſopra il vincitor, che in trionfale
Guerriera pompa del ſanguigno alloro
Cinto la fronte, e da i ſpumanti tratto
Generoſi Corſieri il ſacro clivo
Salìa faſtoſo, de' più ſcelti fiori
D' Elicona verſavi un aureo nembo.
Se dalla ſteſſa amica Terra, adeſſo
Quanto cangiata ahime! lice ad un figlio
Or della ſerva Italia il tuo favore

Power most beneficent, most dear to man,
Bestows upon her sons, and which can raise
The humblest mortals to a rank divine.
For O! one ray from her, gives the free mind
Impulsive ardour of sublimest daring,
Or sweetest song to celebrate the brave.
Come Goddess! thou, who erst th' Italian plains
Did'st ofttimes love to visit, and admire
Prolific virtue there exulting reign:
Thou, who so oft with rapid pinion, flew
O'er the Tarpeian rock, and Latian hills,
To view the fetter'd kings, with front inclin'd,
The vanquish'd German sullenly dismay'd,
And the proud Parthian deck'd with barb'rous gold,
In long-drawn pomp pass thro' the streets of Rome.
While the swift Rhine, the Tigris, and Euphrates,
In mingled semblance tore their sedge-crown'd tresses,
And show'd a broken urn; then all around
Rose the gay Poean, and the loud applause,
As up the sacred hill the victor came
Triumphant, on his valiant brows were bound
The well-earn'd laurels, and his burnish'd car
Four gen'rous Coursers drew with foaming rage.
While o'er his head, thy lib'ral hand diffus'd
An od'rous cloud of Heliconian flowers.
O! from these plains, alas! how sadly changed;

Chiedere, e ofar coll' inefperto labbro
Dar debil fiato alla fublime tromba,
Odimi o Diva, o fe l'antico nido,
E i degeneri figli, or prendi a fdegno,
Deh non fuggire: odimi, i forti carmi
Sacri alla Libertà facri al, valore
Io non profano, ed a cantar ti chiamo
D' Italia nò, ma d' Albione un figlio.

E Tu Signor della tranquilla oliva
Cinto la nobil fronte, che di Temi
Libri con ferma man la facra lance
Sulla torbida Ibernia, e con foave
Sicuro fren, che dolcemente regge
La vigile Prudenza ora le accefe
Anime impazienti all'ira pronte
Moderi e molci, qual fedendo in vetta
Del cavernofo monte i furibondi
Venti lottanti, e i turbini fonori
Eolo raffrena, in lieta fronte accogli
Quefti ch'io vo fpargendo in fulla tomba
Dell'invitto Germano Aonj ferti.
E tu Donna gentil di tanto Spofo
Degna compagna, il cui vago fembiante

If 'tis permitted, for an humble son
Of servile Italy, to claim thy favour;
And dare with lip unhallow'd, and weak breath,
To wake thy awful trumpet, hear me Goddess!
But if perchance, thine eye with proud disdain,
Should view these hills, and vales, if thou should'st scorn
A race degen'rate, yet O! do not fly me.
For ne'er will I profane the manly measure,
Which liberty, and valour may demand:
Then grant me inspiration, while I sing
Nat Italy's, but warlike Albion's son.

O thou illustrious Peer! around whose front
The verdant Olive twines it's peaceful wreath,
Whose hand unshaken bears the balance true
Of sacred Themis, midst Ibernia's rage;
Whose moderation calms her generous sons:
As, on the summit of his mountain drea,
Sits Oeolus, and checks the frantic blast,
And bids the ruthless tempest ceafe to roar:
O deign with eye benignant to behold
This humble garland of Parnaffian flowers,
Which for thy valiant Brother's tomb I weave.
And thou his lovely Consort! heavenly fair!
Whom Nature forming, copied every grace
From the enchanting Queen of smiles, and loves.

B

Quando formò null'altro fe Natura
Che ricopiar della più vaga Dea
Fedelmente il ritratto, e fol vi traffe
Su di modeftia maeftofo velo,
E poi dubbio lafciò fe fien maggiori
I pregi del tuo fpirto o del tuo volto,
Se in udir come i marzìali allori
Del Giovinetto Eroe tingonfi alfine
Di glcriofo fangue, e col funebre
Cipreffo intefti a coronar fen vanno
L'intempeftiva tomba, una dolente
Lacrimetta s'affaccia a i neri lumi,
Trattienla, o Donna illuftre, ah l'onorato
Suo fin degno è d'invidia, e non di pianto.
O Nutrice d'Eroi, madre feconda
Di tutte le virtù dell' arti belle
Anglia, nel di cui feno incerta errante
La combattuta Libertà Latina
Depofe i fafci, e il lacerato manto
Ricomponendo, e la negletta chioma,
Riprefe il fafto ufato, e franca e lieta
D'Aftrea s'affife al non temuto fianco,
Anglia, ed è ver che dell'incauta Figlia,
Figlia che omai fdegna il materno impero,
In altro cielo ed in ftraniero lido
Or muovi irata a lacerare il feno?

And heightened all by winning modefty.

Nor can the world aftonifh'd e'er decide

If more thy perfon, or thy mind excell.

O! should a pearly drop bedew thy cheek,

To view the laurels of th' heroic youth,

With Cyprefs mingled, and diftain'd with gore;

Chafe from thy radiant eyes the cryftal woe,

His death demands our envy, not our tears.

O fruitful Parent of the noblef arts

And all the brighteft virtues, England! ftill

The nurfe of genuine heroes; on thy breaft

Now, long unfettled Roman Liberty

Has placed the mighty fafces of her fway:

Her flowing mantle, and dishevell'd hair,

All readjufted show their wonted glory;

While at her fide Aftraea fmiles ferene.

Alas! dear Britain! thy untoward child

Contemns a gentle mother's foft controul;

In other climates, and on diftant shores,

E fia pur ver ch' oggi l'incauta figlia
Sdegni il materno non fevero freno?
I bruni abitator del nuovo mondo
Scuotonfi al rauco fuon d'armi e di grida,
Onde rifuona il già tranquillo albergo
Del manfueto Cittadin (a) che traffe
La pacifica induftria, e la contenta
Aurea mediocrità da i rumor fi
Lidi d'Europa a un altro mondo in grembo.
O Madre! O Figlia! ah deponete il fiero
Il facrilego brando: e le communi
Leggi, i figli communi, i nomi fteffi
Vi difarmin le deftre: ah non fia vero,
Ah non fia ver che il cor vi ferri e induri
Marte feroce, e a guerre orride guerre
Vi fpinga, guerre di trionfo prive:
Guerre per cui fopra il cognato fangue
Gema egualmente il vincitore, e il vinto:
Roma vide così con mefto ciglio
Quinci di Mitridate il vincitore
De' vecchi cinto, quafi aridi allori,
Quindi fuperbo per la Gallia doma
E i novelli trofei, nè dal fatale
Rubicon trattenuto il fuo più grande

(a) Il Cav. Penn

She now compells thee with unwilling force
To wound her bosom, yet incautious child!
Nor was the Empire so disdain'd severe.
Now too the din of arms, and rage of war,
Wake the brown native of the new-found world,
Nor spare the mild abode of placid Penn,
Who brought from busy Europe's coasts afar,
Industrious labour, and the golden mean,
To spread their influence o'er a peaceful land.
O hapless Mother! Child ingrate! depose
The sacrilegious brand; for sim'lar laws,
And self-same Origin, should surely give
A fond affection, and bid wrath subside.
Nor be it true that your contracted hearts
Excite to fierce alarms of bloody Mars;
For O! no triumph crowns a civil war;
But in a kindred contest, grief awaits
Alike the vanquish'd, and the conqueror.
Rome thus of old, dejectedly beheld
The mighty victor of stern Mithridates
With ancient and with arid laurels crown'd
Advancing here, while there the lord of Gaul,
Proud of new trophies, scorn'd th'indignant bound

E più funesto figlio in fiera pugna
Azzuffarsi feroci, e quinci e quindi
Muover le pari insegne, e il grave pilo
Portare e riportar vide la morte;
Vide, e omai certa dell'estremo fato
La Libertà Latina in negro ammanto
L'Augusta faccia involse, e a lei girando
Fin dall' Elisie sedi i lumi tinti
D'atro livor del Barbaro Anniballe
Rise l'invendicata ombra feroce:
E là dove bevendo il lungo oblio
Stavano ansiose, ed affrettando il lento
Volger de' tardi secoli le nuove
Alme future e i rai del dì dovute (*a*)
Corse, al truce Alarico, al furibondo
Attila, e alle minori ombre dal Fato
Promesse a i Geti ed a i Bistonj boschi
Mostrò i latini Colli, e l'inimiche
Sponde del Tebro, e di sanguigna face
Per man d'Aletto in Flegetonte accesa
Alle terribili ombre armò la destra.

(*a*).. Animae quibus altera fato
   Corpora debentur, Lethei ad fluminis undam
   Securos latices, & longa oblivia potant
                                    Virgil. vi. *Aeneid*.

Of the dread Rubicon; she saw that son,
Her pride, aud terrour, wage abhorred war,
While her own eagled ensigns, and the Pilum
Contending mingled in the fields of death.
Then Latian liberty, her visage hid
In mantle dark, as conscious of her fall.
And the dire shade of barb'rous Hannibal
With eye remorseless gazed on mighty Rome
And felt the rage of Envy; as he stood
On Lethe's borders; suddenly he smiled,
Then sought th' expecting souls of future years,
Who drank th'oblivious stream, who wished in vain
With wild impatience still to hasten on
The tardy progress of succeeding ages.
Fierce Alaric was there, and many a Hero
Of humbler fame, whom destiny had promised
To the rude Gothic, or the Scythian tribes.
He points to these where rise the Roman hills,
And shows them Tyber's shores, then gives to each
A fatal torch, by stern Alecto lighted
In the red stream of flaming Phlegeton.

Ma mentre io parlo invan le ferree porte
Si spalancan di Giano alto stridendo
Su i rugginosi cardini suonanti.
Udite qual dalle funeste soglie
Esce cupo rimbombo? accenti d'ira
„ Parole di dolor, voci alte, e fioche,
„ Diverse lingue, orribili favelle.
Forman di mille suoni insiem confusi
Un fremito indistinto: appunto come
La nascente tempesta da lontano
Con suono ognor più alto romoreggia;
Cresce intorno il fragor: odo i nitriti
De fumanti corsieri, odo il canoro
Guerriero carme della rauca tromba.
Vedete? già fuor delle schiuse soglie
L' infausto Carro di Bellona appare:
Quattro destrier vie più che pece neri
Con occhi accesi e scarmigliati crini
Sbalzano fuor dell'antro, e impazienti
Sbuffando van precipitosi al basso:
Stringe l'atroce Dea l' asta fatale
In atto di ferir: sul gran cimiero
S'ergon di rabbia gonfie e di veleno
Le stigie serpi, e la trisulca lingua
Sibila lampeggiando: al carro avanti
Con irte chiome e spalancati lumi

Whilſt thus I vainly ſpeak, the awful gates
Of Ianus open wide, and with dire ſound,
Upon their rugged hinges grating turn.
Hark! how tumultuous diſcord roars within!
What bitter plaints of uuavailing woe!
What various tongues! that midſt corroding flames
Send furious forth the accents of deſpair.
While from a thouſand murmurs indiſtinɛt,
Is formed one louder murmur, more confuſed.
So on the black Horizon's diſtant bound
Majeſtic thunder rolls the mutt'ring peal,
The Din encreaſes, high and boaſtful neighings
Anſwer the brazen trumpet's warlike ſong.
And from the portal ſtern Bellona comes,
Her iron Chariot drawn by ſable ſteeds,
With flaming eye-balls, and with ruffled manes.
Impatient of controul, they onward ruſh,
To quit the dreary ſcene, and dark abode.
The ſhouting Goddeſs lifts her fatal lance
In aɛt to ſtrike, and o'er her burniſh'd helm
Fierce ſtygian ſnakes riſe tow'ring like a Plume;
That hiſs with forked tongues, and venom'd rage.
Before the Car, pale terrour madly runs

Il gelido Terror pallido in volto
Corre, e quanto più corre ognor s' accrefce
E gigante fi fa: corteggio infame
La rapina l'orror l'odio il furore
Girano intorno, e poi feguita il carro
Con cave tempie, ed infoffati lumi
L' eftenuata fame, e infin ne viene
Lenta la folitudine penfofa.
Tartarea nube e più che notte nera
Involve il carro: ma il fanguigno lume
Delle ferrate rote che sfavillano
Qual di fornace ardente ignito ferro .
Allora tratto, gl' occhi furibondi
Della Dea, che roffeggian quai fiammanti
Minacciofe comete, il vafto fcudo
Che di focofa luce folgorante
Emula il Sol, quando ful lembo eftremo
Dell'orizonte in vaporofo velo
Cade ravvolto, della negra nube
Che cinge il carro il tenebrofo manto
Tingono d' atro lume: in aere fcoppia
Il vipereo flagello onde l' Auriga
Aletto sferza i fervidi deftrieri.
Appena efcita dall' ofcure porte
Alza la Diva un formidabil grido
Che chiama all' armi, e tofto in aria fcaglia
L' afta fatale; all'armi all'armi s' ode

With hair uplifted, and enanguish'd look,
Till in his flight a giant's form he wears.
There follow too, grim horrour, pensive grief,
Relentless cruelty, her heart of stone,
Eye-sunken famine, and to fill the band,
With ling'ring step sad solitude behind.
Tartarean smoke involves the bounding wheels,
Whose rapid course emits a blood-like flame,
As the keen furnace pours the fiery steel.
Where'er the Goddess throws her frantic glance,
A Comet seems to blaze, and her broad shield,
Like day's red Orb when sinking in the west;
Glows with dim lustre thro'a vap'rous veil.
The Chariot glimm'ring from the livid light,
Alecto drives, and o'er th' indignant steeds,
With Hell's own fury shakes a scorpion scourge.

4.

Loud in her course enraged Bellona cries,
To arms, to arms, and hurls her thirsty spear,
To arms, to arms, hills, woods, and vales resound.

Con ſtrepitoſo fremito confuſo
Echeggiar da ogni parte: il ſol coprio
Di ſcuro velo il luminoſo crine
Si ſcoſſe il ſuol; tremò natura, e al ſeno
Strinſer le Madri i pargoletti Figli,
Sibilò l'aſta rapida pe' voti
Aerei campi, e di fulminea luce
Dietro ſi traſſe un fuggitivo lampo:
Qual di ſerena notte il foſco manto
Segna talor con paſſaggiero lume
Vapore acceſo: al mar d'Atlante in ſeno
Cadde l'aſta ſanguigna, e appena tocco
L'ondoſo piano che in ſoave calma
Dormìa tranquillo, in vorticoſi giri
Si ſconvolge mugghiando: onda con onda
S'urta ſi rompe, le ſpumoſe e bianche
Cime inalzando al Ciel: dalle ſpezzate
Eolie grotte ſprigionati i venti
Miſchiano ſcompigliando e l'aria e l'onda,
Sopra delle cui teſte il nero carro
Pende e ſi muove alle lor penne ſopra
Tra le folgori torte e i tuoni involto,
Già del Tamigi e della Senna i fieri
Emuli figli in minaccioſa fronte
Si disfidano all'armi, e quai dal teſo
Canape della tromba al primo ſquillo

Meantime. the sun his golden treßes hides
In dusky mantle, earth's dry bosom quakes,
All Nature sickens, and each mother strains
Fond, to her throbbing heart the tim'rous babe.
The thirsty spear that cleaves the liquid air,
And marks it's course with train of lucid fire;
(As streams the glitt'ring meteor of the night)
Deep in th'e vast Atlantic sinks at last.
Sudden the waves, then hush'd in calm repose,
Dash angry round, and curl their foam to heaven,
While winds swift bursting from Aeolian caves,
Midst the grim hurricane, and the vengeful storm,
Bear the enraged Bellona's fiery car.

Now the embattled sons of Thames, and Seine,
Rush hasty forward to the conflict dire;
As eager coursers starting for the prize,

Con arruffato pelo e con fpumofe
Labbra slancianfi i barberi anelanti
Nel vuoto arringo sì, che dallo fpeffo
Urto delle fonanti ugne veloci
Crolla il terreno, e polverofa nube
E gl'involge, e gli fegue: in afpro vòlto
Così gl'emuli altieri aprono il corfo
Alle belliche prore, che di cavi
Fulminei bronzi e di velate antenne
Con minacciofa pompa alto torreggiano.
Ma fra cotanti Eroi che dal tuo facro
Di libertade albergo, Anglia faftofa,
Lieti mandafti a foftener col fangue
I dritti tuoi, quale ornerem primiero
Dell'Aonie ghirlande? o Giovinetto
De i Manners vetufti almo rampollo,
In sì tenera età gl'atroci rifchi
Corri a sfidar di Marte? Il curvo Pino
Porta il giovine Eroe, frefca dipinge
Giovinezza e beltà la vaga guancia
Che rofea fplende, e amabile, ne ancora
Della prima lanugine fi vefte:
Ma l'immatura età fenno virile
Spirti generofi, alma capace
Di gloriofa morte in fen racchiude
Ed il valore, e la virtù che appare

When the shrill trumpet gives the sprightly sound,
With manes wide waving, and with foamy rage,
Dart o'er the plain, while to their rattl'ing hoofs,
The firm soil sounds, and rolling clouds arise.
So the contending rivals for fair fame,
Induce their course, they guide their floating towers
O'er the rough waves, and spread the whit'ning sails,
While Death prepares the yawning throats of war.

But O! for whom of all the gen'rous tribe
That left thy coast, where liberty resides,
Proud Albion! say? for whom I first shall weave
Th' Aonian garland, since so many strove
To save thine honour, and defend thy rights?
Intrepid Manners, Granby's gallant son,
In life's gay prime now sought the bloody scene,
And breathed defiance to the raging Mars.
Stern on his vessel's dauntless prow he stood,
While o'er his cheek warm glow'd the pride of youth,
Refulgent hue of Nature's early bloom.
Tho on his lip but scarce the down appear'd,
Yet manly sense, and vigour, fired his breast;
Honour he most adored, and his bold heart
Alike disdain'd pale fear, or paler death.

Ancor più bella in un leggiadro volto.
Ei le primizie della fresca etade
Non al piacer che con inganno alletta,
Ma di Marte a i perigli alle fatiche
Confacrò generofo; al fuon guerriero
Di color d' ardimento ei fi dipinge.
Mentre mugghiando più e più s'annera
La marzìal tempefta, ecco che denfo
Di guerra un nembo impetuofo forge
Dalle Galliche fponde, ed in fembiante
Non men feroce verfo lui s' avanza
Da i lidi oppofti d' Albion fdegnofo
Il Turbine guerriero: il mar frappofto
Alle nemiche terre i primi vide
Sanguinofi preludj (a) ove in incerto
Ed indecifo agon quafi a far prova
Di forza s' incontrar gl'emuli altieri.
Tal due Tori falvatici che irrita
Furor gelofo, pria che in ftretta pugna
Urtin le fronti, minacciofi in atto
Lenti lenti s' apprefſano, e le luci
Volgonfi accefe e più che bragia roffe,
Spargon col piè l' arena, ai duri tronchi
L' aguzze corna arruotano, ed il vano
Aer ferendo sfidanfi col roço

(a) La battaglia d' Oveffaint data il dì 27. Lug. 1778.

Virtue, in graceful form, enchants the more.
Valiant, and great, He lavish'd not his time
In flow'ry pleasures, nor in wanton joy;
But midst the thunder of rude battle came,
E'en like a God, and there sedately brave,
Gazed on the perils of destructive war.
Now, from the Gallic shores, a gath'ring storm
Of vengeance threatens; Albion's chalky cliffs
Send forth an uproar wild, with equal rage.
The roaring billows, that divide the land,
Witness th' approaching tumult, while the ships
With awful presage seem to practise war,
And doubtful conquest waits the em'lous fight.
So two fierce bulls, by jealous fury driven,
Ere yet in close attack their foreheads join,
Pause with slow pace, and meditate destruction;
Indignant roll their eyes, they beat the ground,
And whet their pointed horns er ev'ry tree;
Rend the thin air, and bellow proud defiance,
While list'ning Echo answers to the sound.

C

Ch'empie le selve e i monti atro mugito.
Il mio Giovin guerrier dal primo illustre
Saggio qual chiuda marzìale ardore
Entro del sen dimostra, e che la tarda
Opra non son del Tempo i veri Eroi.
Ma di Marte il fragore ognor più cresce
E più s'avanza, e il generoso Ibero
Che guarda ancor con onta e con dispetto
Di Calpe un tempo sua l'erto dirupo,
A cui natura insuperabil cinse
Muro d' onde e di scogli, in doppio assalto
E dal suolo, e dall' onda a lui si scaglia:
Gl'impavidi Guerrier dall'alta cima
Miran sicuri invan battuto il sasso
Da' folgori di guerra: appunto come
Olimpo vede dall'eccelsa vetta
Sotto di se di negre nubi in seno
Ardere i lampi, e strepitare il tuono.
Ma con pallida faccia, e lenti colpi
Contro i chiusi guerrier tacita pugna
Muove la fame, del nemico porto
Con minacciosa d'armi ampia catena
Serra ogni varco, e il suo trionfo aspetta.
Volgono i chiusi Eroi gl'avidi sguardi
Verso l'amica terra, e di soccorso

'Twas now th' impatient Warriour firſt diſplay'd
Sublimeſt courage in his country's cauſe;
And proved that valour can excite the young,
Nor needs the aid of lazy pacing time.

Loud yells the voice of war, and diſcord doubles;
Imperious Spain, with shame, and anger, views
Th' iuſulting height of Calpe, once her own,
By nature fortified with rocks, and waves.
Here then she points her long-contending force,
While, on the ſummit placed, the warlike tribe
Mark her mad fury ſpend itſelf in vain;
So tall Olympus ſees the light'nings flash,
And hears the midway thunder roar beneath,
Thro the dull boſom of encircling clouds:
But raging Famine, with her viſage wan,
Anguish unſpeakable, and ſilent ſtep,
Scowls like a fiend upon th' impriſon'd Heroes,
And binds her chain around; she thus impedes
All entrance to the ports, and waits her triumph:
Meantime th' encircled band with eager eyes

Le apportatrici fofpirate vele
Affrettan col defio. Ma quale afcolto
Strepito d'armi? In denfo fumo involte
Odo tuonar fulminee prore: io miro
Errar fopra il fanguigno ondofo piano
E rotte antenne e lacerate vele.
Vedete in fen della guerriera nube
Tutto il fuoco marzìale accefo
Il Giovinetto Eroe col petto audace
Volare incontro a i fulmini di Morte?
Ma già libero è il varco, e le nemiche
Vele qual fugge, e quale il prigioniero
Veffillo abbaffa: diffipata al fine
La fumofa caligine di Marte;
Ecco apparir ful formidabil pino
D'Anglia il foftegno, alla cui chioma intorno
L'avito allor più bello oggi rinverde
Ecco Rodney: fulla guerriera fronte
L'intrepid'alma rimirate pinta,
E l'ardente valor, che col maturo
Senno congiunto fopra il grave fguardo,
E tra le rughe del fevero ciglio
Sta nobilmente impreffo; egli al novello
Giovin guerrier volge benigni i lumi:
Qual feroce Leon, che dopo il fiero
Sanguinofo contrafto in cui difperfe

Gaze on the wat'ry plain, and wish to see
From Britain's isle the succ'ring ships arrive.
But O! what sounds now rush upon mine ear!
The noise of battle hurtles in the air;
Hoarse cannons pierce the smoky clouds of war;
And rent sails, mingl'ing with the shatter'd masts,
In wild disorder float upon the deep.
Here all serene th' aspiring Hero came,
His lib'ral heart, with martial ardour fired,
Scoff'd at grim danger, and oppofing death.
Again the entrance free, the adverse fleet
Secure their safety by inglorious flight;
While yielded vessels prove Iberia's shame.
At length, the smoky gloom of Mars dispell'd,
Upon his formidable deck appears
The living bulwark of Britannia's fame,
Around whose brow the antient laurel seems,
E'en now, to send a greener lustre forth.
'Tis Rodney; lo! upon his martial front,
Amid his serious gaze, and frown severe,
Is mark'd th'intrepid sterness of his soul,
Exalted valour, settled judgment too.
He turns his eyes upon the warlike youth,
As the grim Lion when the battle's o'er,

E ſteſe al ſuolo i Cacciator Numidi,
Mira il piccol figlio, a cui non anco
Pendon dal giovin collo i duri velli,
Che ardito venne all'inegual cimento
Non ſperato compagno, e col mal fermo
Dente lacera già le palpitanti
Membra, e il ſangue ſul labro avido ſugge:
Tale il gran Duce il mira, e premio degno
A quel valor d'un Anglico veſſillo,
Che quaſi lieto di ſua nuova ſorte
Sull' alta antenna alteramente ondeggia,
Il fà cuſtode, e il torreggiante legno,
Di duplice di bronzi ordine cinto
Quaſi a guerrier maturo a lui confida. (a)
Le vincitrici prore al non più chiuſo
Amico porto già drizzano il corſo
Fra i novelli trofei, già le ſaluta
Dal lido oppoſto un mormorìo giulivo,
Che intorno echeggia, e d'allegrezza un tuono
„ Che fremer l'aria, e rimbombar fa l'onde,

(a) Il valore con cui Lord Manners ſi portò nell'a-
zione preſſo Gibilterra ove reſtò vinto e preſo D. Gio-
vanni Langarà, fu ammirato dal celebre Rodney a ſe-
gno che ſubito dopo l'azione lo fece Capitano della
Nave di 74. pezzi di Cannone detta la *Riſoluzione*.

With the Numidian hunters, far dispersed,
Or torn in pieces; views his dauntless young,
Unmaned as yet, who full of boldness came,
All unexpected to th'unequal fight:
Pleased he beholds him tear some tremb'ling limbs
With early tooth, and drink the flowing blood.
So look'd the glorious chief, and in reward
Promoted to a flag the valiant youth.
The floating fortress proudly cuts the tide,
And joyful waves it's honours from the mast,
And now to him, as to a vet'rans care,
The double row of brazen guns is given.
Lo! where the conq'ring vessels bend their course,
Midst their new trophies, to the friendly port
No longer shut, while, on the jocund shore,
Is heard the loud salute of murm'ring joy,
That echoes round midst roaring winds, and waves,
While the triumphant voice of hollow cannon
Joins with the clam'rous seamen's wild applause:

A cui di plaufo tra feftofe grida
De' cavi bronzi il trionfal mugito
Lieto rifponde, e il nautico clamore.
Allor là dove dell'invitto fcoglio
Al piè fi frange l'Ocean fpumante,
Che dell'angufta via quafi fdegnofo
Europa e Libia urta sferzando, e caccia
L'oppofto mare, e lo foverchia e inonda;
Gonfio più dell'ufato ergerfi in alto
Fù vifto un flutto, e poich'in vafti giri
In fe fteffo fi torfe, alfin s'aprìo,
E dal ceruleo grembo in fovrumana
Orrida maeftà forfe l'antico
Genio cuftode del temuto varco,
Genio che già la provida Natura
Vi pofe in guardia a raffrenar l'infano
Ardimento mortale, e fopra i venti
I nembi e le procelle a lui conceffe
Formidabile impero; il fuo potere
Alcide rifpettò, l'audace Uliffe,
Che l'onda ignota osò tentar, fi giacque
Ingoiato da' vortici fpumanti:
Ma l'ira fua fatal, la fua poffanza
Sprezzaro al fine il Lufitano ardito,
Ed il Ligure Tifi; egli l'antico
Regno, e il terror del nome fuo perdpto

Here, *where the haughty ocean dashing fierce*
Against the rock invincible, *appears*
To scorn the narrow pass, *and proudly beats*
Europe and Lybia, *with indignant force*,
Sudden the curling waters rage, *und swell*,
And break in foamy volumes; wide they ope
A horrid chasm, *from whence uprising slow*,
In dread, *sublime*, *and hoary majesty*,
The guardian Genius of the straits is seen;
Genius, *whom nature wise*, *and provident*,
Here placed to check the hardy enterprize
Of daring mortals, *to whom pow'r was given*
Over the whirlwind's speed, *and howling storm*.
Him great Alcides reverenc'd, *but Ulysses*,
Who scorning dared to tempt the unknown sea,
Was overwhelm'd beneath the frothy surge.
At length the bold aspiring Lusitanian,
And the Ligurian Tiphis, *mock'd his ire*,
So fatal once, *and all his power disdain'd:*
Since then, *his empire o'er*, *dethron'd*, *and sad*,
The gloomy Monarch, *in his cave obscure*,
Neglected, *and inglorious*, *passed his day*.

Qual detronato Re nell'antro ofcuro
Ora negletto e ingloriofo giace.
Ma dal lungo letargo a i lieti gridi
Di gioia, e di vittoria allor fi fcoffe,
„ E qual albero in nave fi levò
Dall'ondeggiante letto; ei nuota in mezzo
Al cupo mare, eppur gli bagna l'onda
Appena il fianco : allorch' ei muove il paffo
Sorgono accanto a lui fpumofi e rotti
I flutti come da Aquilon commoffi :
Di ramofo corallo, e di ritorte
Argentee conche intefto un ampio ferto
Gli cinge il crin, la verde barba algofa
Stilla grondante ful limofo petto,
Stringe a triplice antenna eguale il facro
Luminofo tridente: il raggio intanto
Del fol che fere e la ftillante chioma,
E i coralli, e le conche, e i fpruzzi acquofi,
Che rugiadofa a lui fpargono intorno
Nebbia fottile, in colorate ftrifce
Quinci e quindi fi rompe, e fcherza e cinge
D'Iride il volto al Nume, e lo ravvolge
Tutto in divina maeftofa luce.

Now, at the shout of joyful victory,

From his long lethargy he rises slow

As in a vessel towers the haughty mast;

So from the Ocean's dreary depth he comes,

And while he wades amid the briny flood,

The white wave throws it's curling fury round.

As tho the raging south-wind drove the storm.

His front sustain'd an ample diadem,

Where richest shells, and branching coral shone;

A sedgy beard fell verdant on his breast,

Besmear'd with mud, and there in drops distill'd;

He bore the sacred trident of his reign

That seem'd a triple mast, the sun's bright beam

Play'd on his humid locks, and glitt'ring crown,

While chrystal drops the many-colour'd rays

Resplendent broke, and like a circling Iris

Enwrap'd his head with noblest majesty.

Pieni di facro orrore alzan la fronte
Attoniti i guerrieri: il nume allora,
Qual dalle rotte nubi fi fprigiona
Il rimbombante mormorar del tuono,
In fatidiche voci il labbro aperfe.
O Figli d' Albion Figli felici
Dell'alma Libertà, quella che fpira
Penfier fublimi e più fublimi imprefe,
Che infegna a viver grandemente, e infieme
Grandemente a morir, voi che chiudete
Alme Romane entro Britanni petti,
E degni fiete che vi parli un Nume,
Guerrieri illuftri andate ove v'appella
Della Patria l'onor, la gloria voftra ;
Di Nettunno e di Marte ite lo fdegno
Ad affrontare: oh qual nell'agitata
Urna il deftino al voftro alto valore
Sorte illuftre prepara! io veggio io veggio
Rotto e fanguigno a voi davanti il giglio:
Veggio le femivive e palpitanti
Membra ondeggiar ne' flutti, il lembo eftremo,
Che co' cadenti raggi il fole indora
Del mar d'Atlante è colorato in roffo.
O Duce invitto al tuo valore è dato
Il ricompor nel vacillante trono,
Che a lei fe l'ampio mar Nettunno diede,

Th' aftonish'd warriours ftruck with horrour, raife
Their valiant fronts, when now the Deity,
Like hollow thunder burfting from the clouds,
In slow, and awful murmurs thus began.
,, *O fons of Albion! happieft offspring dear*
,, *Of facred liberty, that knows t' infpire*
,, *Sublimeft thoughts, and glorious enterprize;*
,, *Of facred liberty, whofe leffons teach*
,, *Greatly to live, and more, to greatly die :*
,, *O fons of Albion! ye have Roman fouls,*
,, *And well deferve a God fhould thus addrefs you.*
,, *Illuftrious Heroes! go where honour calls,*
,, *Far from your grateful Country's fertile plains,*
,, *To dare old Ocean, and the Lord of war.*
,, *Your val'rous deeds, and defliny renown'd,*
,, *Within the pregnant Urn of fate I fee;*
,, *At your approach, the Gallic lily shows*
,, *A bloodlike tint, and droops her forrowing head;*
,, *Amid the waves, with palpitations dire*
,, *Float the half-living limbs, and the far shores*
,, *Of the Atlantic, where the Orb of light*
,, *Throws his declining ray is tinged with red.*
,, *Rodney invincible! to thee 'tis given,*
,, *Again to fix on Neptune's tott'ring throne,*

La combattuta Patria, e far che fegga
De Regni ondofi ancor Donna e Reina.

Vanne, dell'arbor facra e trionfale
Che rigogliofa un dì fulle guerriere
Fiorì fponde del Tebro, arbor felice,
,, Che per lunga ftagion foglia non perde,
Serto immortal prepara alla tua fronte
Già la Vittoria; oh valorofo Duce
Grande, e più grande ancor, fe il bianco fguardo
Dell'invidia non temi: ah l'impotente
Rabbiofo mormorar fprezza; e fublime
,, Non ti curar di lui ma guarda e paffa.

E tu nobil Garzone, a cui nel feno
Di gloria, e di virtù l'impaziente
Fiamma anzi tempo bolle, e in immatura
Età ti tragge ful fentiero illuftre
Degl'avi tuoi guerrieri: oh fe la legge
La ferrea legge in adamante fcritta
Romper poteffi, e l'invincibil fato, (a)
Qual terrore il nemico, e qual foftegno
La Patria avria! non mai dal fen fecondo
Dell'Anglia a tanta fpeme altro mai forfe
Generofo rampollo: oh dal crudele
Deftino a noi moftrato appena e tolto!
Ma voi le molli mie querule voci

(a) Si qua fata afpera rumpas
    Tu Marcellus eris.

„ *Your injured country, and to make her reign,*

„ *Unrival'd Empress of the watry world.*

„ *Go then brave leader, where new wreaths await thee,*

„ *Fair wreaths, collected from that well-known tree,*

„ *Which grew of old on yellow Tyber's shore,*

„ *And whose green leaves for ages ne'er shall fade.*

„ *For thou art great, and hadst been greater too,*

„ *But that the jaundic'd eye of envy scowls*

„ *To tarnish all thy fame, O then despise*

„ *Each mean, and jealous murmur, but bestow*

„ *In conscious virtue safe, a passing smile.*

„ *And thou too, noblest youth! whose bosom feels*

„ *Th' impatient glow of valour, and of fame,*

„ *Nor yet mature in age, where battle calls,*

„ *Canst emulate thy martial Ancestors:*

„ *O! where it possible to break the laws,*

„ *The adamantine laws of ruthless fate,*

„ *Amazed futurity had seen thee rise*

„ *Thy country's bulwark, and her foe's despair,*

„ *For never yet has fruitful England borne*

„ *So fair a hope, nor youth so justly dear;*

„ *By destiny a moment shewn, and lost.*

„ *But you must scorn my weak, and quer'lous lay,*

Sdegnate o Prodi: udite il lieto carme
Che intuona già la Fama? a voi davante
Volar vedeſte con purpuree penne
Ed agitar le tremule bandiere
La Vittoria ſegnando a voi la ſtrada?
Ite che già v'aſpetta, e à in man la palma.
Diſſe, e battendo colle ſteſe braccia
L'azzurro pian, la china fronte, e il curvo
Doſſo naſcoſe in ampio tuffo, e ſparve:
Balzò l'onda percoſſa in alti ſpruzzi,
E fluttuando ſopra lui ſi chiuſe.
I promeſſi trofei novello ardire
Porgono alle alme forti: e tu frattanto
O Giovinetto a cui con negra mano
Contando i brevi dì la Sorte accenna
Che fai? forſe nel cor poteo l'ardente
Guerriero foco la crudel minaccia
Intiepidire? O gloria! oh la più bella
Mercè delle gentili alme! oh del ſaggio
Ultima debolezza! di quel baſſo
Pregio è la vita incontro a te! ſi ſcorda
L'Uomo per te d'eſſer mortale, e guarda
La morte anche immatura come un varco,
Che d'immortalità lo guida al Tempio.
Tremino i vili, a cui torvo la fronte
Si preſenta ogn'iſtante il Fato eſtremo
Con gelato ribrezzo: eſſi nel breve

,, *Lift .. the louder jong of shouting fame,*

,, *Behold before you on her purple wing,*

,, *Flies blooming Vict'ry and points the way,*

,, *Go where she waits you now, and shows the palm.*

,, *He spoke, and sudden beat the azure flood*

,, *With outftrecht arms, then with his front inclin'd,*

,, *And curving back, plung'd to his deep abode.*

The troubled waters dash their foam on high,

And then ferene in dimpling eddies close.

Meantime the promifed trophies roufe them all

To new exploits, and valour fires their fouls.

But thou brave youth! alas! whom fate's dark hand

Has rudely mark'd, (fo thy short day shall prove)

Say what doft thou? too fure thy dauntlefs heart

Difdains to tremble at the cruel menace:

Thou feek'ft for glory, beft reward of minds

Gen'rous like thine, laft weaknefs of the wife,

Compared to which, how poor this little life!

Thro' Glory man forgets his mortal doom,

And thinks of coming death without a fear.

For tis the road that leads his footfteps on,

To the bright fane of immortality.

But they who shake whene'er the grisly king

Threatens with ebon rod, and angry gaze;

Conftrain'd by icy fear, in life's short hour,

D

Giro degl'anni muojon mille volte.
Sparita è Calpe, e le vittrici prore
Corrono a nuove imprefe. O voi di Giove
Canore Figlie, dite, e chi fu quegli,
Che primo vide il fluttuante al vento
Giglio difefo invan da doppio giro
Di fulmini guerrieri a fe davante
Abbaffarfi, e cader? Tu fofti invitto
Giovine Eroe: (*a*) dalle lontane arene
La Patria il vide, e di feftofo plaufo
Suonaro i Lidi d'Albione e i Colli.
Solca il Pino guerrier l'azzurro feno
Del placido Nettunno, a lui d'intorno
Spianan l'onde tranquille il curvo dorfo:
Zeffiro fcherza, e le lafcive penne
Gode agitar fra le vittrici infegne.
Ride fereno il Cielo, e dà mufcofi
Antri, e dall'onde fuori ergon la fronte
Ed Anfitrite e Galatea con mille
Nereidi, verdi le ftillanti treccie,

(*a*) Lord Manners appena fatto Capitano del Va-
fcello di Linea la *Rifoluzione*, prefe combattendo Legno con Legno, la Nave di Linea Francefe il *Proteo*, che
fu la prima Nave di Linea prefa in quefta guerra
dagl'Inglefi.

Must die a thousand times a living death.
Now *Calpe vanish'd, the victorious prows*
   Haste to new dangers, and fresh enterprize.
O *tuneful Daughters of almighty* Iove!
Say, who was he, that saw the lily first
High trembling in the air, to droop, and die,
By warlike thunders guarded but in vain ?
Thou, Thou wast he, unconquerable youth !
Thy country mark'd thee from her distant strand;
And the loud Chorus of sublime applause,
Was heard on Albion's *cliffs, and tow'ring hills.*
The haughty vessel cleaves the azure breast
Of placid Neptune, *whose rough waves subside,*
And gentle Zephyr *shakes his wanton wings*
Midst the victorious ensigns with delight,
The air was calm, and on the level deep
Fair Amphitritè *sported, for she came*
With Galatea *from her pearly grot,*
And thousand Nereids *green, with dropping hair,*

E glauche i vivi lumi, e fopra curve
Dipinte conche affife, il piano ondofo
Radon veloci, come preffo al polo
Sull' indurito flutto in lunghi ftrifci
Le villanelle fdrucciolan ficure:
E al Giovinetto Eroe, che fulla prora
Siede penfofo, e col defire affretta
Il tardo legno, volte, e chi la bionda
Chioma n'ammira, chi le rofee guancie,
Chi di foco guerrier gl'accefi lumi:
E vedendo che lui di pallid'ombra
La ftigia notte già circonda e vela,
Dogliofe goccie, quai perle nafcenti
Spargon dalle pupille: il pianto ifteffo
Verfaro un dì della cerulea Teti
Al Figlio intorno, allorchè abbandonate
Le molli fpoglie, per l'Egeo fpumante
Volava ardito, e fopra il Pin fatale
D'Ilio il deftino, e il fuo portava infieme.
Dove più ferve, ove più irato tuona
Marte alle Spiagge Americane accanto
Di pugna e di vittoria firibonde
Giungon l'Angliche Prore: or chi mai tutte
Ridir potrà tue gloriofe gefta,
Prode Roberto? Non alzò Bellona
Mai ful liquido pian l'atro veffillo

And eyes of glossy blue that sweetly shine;
Reposed on painted shells they gaily skim
In many a mazy course the liquid plain:
So glides the Northern peasant o'er the ice:
On the brave youth they gaze, who pensive sits
Upon his rising deck, and fain would haste
His ship's too tardy progress: some admire
His golden tresses, some his glowing cheek,
Or eyes that sparkle with heroic flame,
And knowing well that stygian night is near,
To wrap him in the universal shade,
In many a lucid tear their pity flows.
And the same grief again they feel, that erst
On the sad son of Thetis they bestow'd,
When, having left his female robes, he sail'd
With daring vessel o'er th' Egeean deep,
And bore his own fate, and the fate of Troy.

Now where stern Mars bids fiercer thunders roar
   Around America's extending coast,
   For Battle eager, and for conquest keen,
   With bulging sail the British fleet appears.
   Ah! who shall tell of all thy glorious deeds
Illustrious youth? still where Bellona raised
   Her sable standard on the rolling wave,

Che fotto lui non affrontaſſi in cento
Modi la morte: io con quel facro lume,
Con cui Febo rifchiara a i fuoi diletti
Vati la mente, a i fibilanti in mezzo
Ferrei globi ti miro, ch'ora il crine (a)
Ti radono, or le piante, e gelo e tremo
Mentre tu fei tranquillo. Ecco che quaſi
Gonfio torrente l'inimico ingroſſa,
E del numero fier con ampio giro
D'affollati veſſilli, ove pompofo
L'aurato giglio folgoreggia al vento,
Circonda e preme l'Anglo ſtuol divifo
Già dall'aura nemica: i mal concordi
Separati fquadron, quaſi dal corpo
Divife membra, più del fommo Duce
Non rimirano i cenni, e nell'opaco
Dubbiofo velo della notte Figlia
Confuſìon le menti e gl'occhi involve.
Or chi farà che alla divifa, incerta,
Confufa fquadra oſi appreſſare, e il cenno
Recar del Duce, fe di morte cinta,
E di Terrore l'inimica fchiera

(a) Più volte Lord Manners è ſtato in procinto
d'eſſere colpito da una palla di Cannone, da cui
una volta gli fu portata via la punta del cappello.

Thou bravely cam'ft to dare a thoufand deaths.

By that all-facred light which Phœbus gives

His favour'd Bards, I view thee fternly ftand,

Where leaden fate in hiffing fhower defcends;

And as the winged dangers fweep around,

Thon art unfhaken, but I fhrink with fear.

Behold the enemy come pouring on,

Like a fwoln torrent numerous, and proud;

The countlefs enfigns form a circ'ling range,

And high the golden lily waves in air.

While they furrounding prefs the British fleet,

By adverfe winds divided, and difperfed;

As members from the body torn, no more

Obey their head, e'en fo Britannia's fons,

Their Adm'ral's fignals now no more obferve.

But wild confufion, dull night's offfpring drear,

With doubtful veil involves their ufelefs fight.

Ah! who shall gain the feperated fleet,

To bear the leader's orders? for the foe

Arm'd with fwift terrour, and impending death,

Sta tuonando framezzo? ecco che quale
L'Augel di Giove per l'aeree ſtrade
Degl'altri augei fra il crocitante ſtuolo
Paſſa ſicuro, e rapido: il veloce
Pino, che guida il Giovinetto ardito (a)
Per vie di ſangue, in mezzo al folto boſco
Delle nemiche antenne entra ſicuro,
E mentre il mira, e appena agl'occhi crede
L'attonito nemico, ei corre e vola,
E giunge a' ſuoi, quaſi celeſte meſſo
Inaſpettato, ed il diſordin cieco
All'apparir di lui, qual d'improviſa
Face al chiaror l'oſcurità, ſi ſcioglie.
Ma il Genio d'Albion l'atra e ſevera
Fronte crollando con acceſi lumi
Sangue chiede, e vendetta, i ſuoi guerrieri
Figli rampogna, a più mortal conflitto
Gli ſpinge, e ad eſſi il non ben vinto ancora
Giglio addita crucioſo, e il guarda e freme,

(a) Queſta non è una finzione poetica, ma un puro
racconto iſtorico di ciò che avvenne in una azione
ne i mari d'America tra i Franceſi, e gl'Ingleſi comandati dall'Ammiraglio Graves.

Have placed their brazen thunder's rage between.

As Jove's eternal Eagle thro' the sky

Sails with supreme dominion, nor regards

The num'rous croakings of surrounding birds:

So ardent Manners—yes 'twas he, that came

Safe midst the crimson slaughter, and a grove

Of threat'ning Masts. Th' astonish'd Enemy

Doubt what they see, while he pursues his course,

And joins his friends, a heavenly messenger.

Soon as approach'd, the wild disorder's o'er,

So from a sudden ray grim darkness flies.

Now Albion's Genius lifts his front severe,

Indignant fire wide flashing from his eyes,

And shouts to vengeance, and excites to blood,

Urges his daring sons to keener fight,

Points the proud lilies not as yet subdued,

Sangue gridando, e *morte*: ed il feroce
Impazìente ſtuol con ſuon concorde
Sangue, ſangue, ululando a lui riſponde.
E già ſull'ali minaccioſe pende .
Il formidabil dì (*a*) doglioſe e lenté
L'ore al fiammante Carro i freni aurati
Vanno avvolgendo, di Titon la Spoſa
Dall'Atlantico mar, dalla vicina
Strage i pietoſi lumi altrove torſe,
E il roſeo volto di pallor dipinſe.
O Sol che ſpunti (*b*) e coll' immenſo ſguardo
Della Terra, e del mare i vaſti giri
Arduo miſuri, vedi in qual ſuperbo
Aſpetto minaccioſo, in qual guerriera
Orrida pompa in' ſulle ali del vento;
Quinci e quindi sfidandoſi ſdegnoſe
Già le rivali ſquadre in ſulle azzurre
Umide vie paſſeggian fiere, e fanno
Vaga e terribil moſtra? Oh Sole allora

(*a*) La battaglia del dì 12.Aprile avvenuta nel 1782. tra le Flotte Ingleſe , e Franceſe ſotto gl'ordini degl' Ammiragli Rodney e Graſſe.

(*b*) Queſta ſanguinoſa battaglia cominciò poco dopo lo ſpuntar del ſole, e terminò poco avanti il tramontare.

And at the fight, shouts more to blood, and death;

While back the squadron echoes blood, and death.

With gloomy frown the low'ring day comes on,

And the sad hours, adjust with tardy care,

The golden reins to guide the flaming car.

Titans lov'd consort turns her melting eyes

Far from th' Atlantic, and th' approaching war.

While on her alter'd cheek the rose is pale.

O rising Sun! who see'st th' immense expanse

Of varied lands, and Ocean's ruffled bed,

Behold in horrid pomp, and eager pride

Th' opposing fleets mutual defiance breathe,

As on the wings of winds they ride the deep.

Che dechinando fuggìrai da queſto
Sventurato orizzonte, ahi come, ahi come
Cambiata tu vedrai la ſcena! oh quanti
Di quei prodi guerrier, che ſulla prora
Ti ſalutan feſtoſi, e il tuo ritorno
Impazìenti affrettano, nell'onda
Non ti vedran cader, nè più per loro
Riſorgerai! bello è il mirar da lungi
D'alberi qùaſi due foreſte annoſe
Quinci e quindi ondeggiare, e quali al cenno
Del duro Capitan l'orride file
De'terreſtri guerrier pronte e veloci
Or s'aprono, or ſi chiudono, ora in lunga
Colonna s'aſſottiglian sì, che pare
Che tante membra mùova un alma ſola:
Tal quelle vaſte moli in mille e mille
Rapidi e varj artificioſi giri
Volteggiano concordi, e già Signore
Dell'aure, che a curvati e teſi lini
Obbediſcon fremendo, ecco che in lungo
Ordin diſteſe appreſſano ſdegnoſe,
E colle aperte inſegne, e colla cupa
Voce de bronzi sfidanſi al conflitto.
Così talor ſe negl'eſtivi ardori
Quinci Auſtro in guerra vien, quindi Aquilone
Muovonſi incontro per gl'aerei campi

O fulgent Sun! ere thy declining ray
Shall leave this sad Horison's distant bound,
How changed shall be the present scene, alas!
What numbers of the brave, and valiant tribe,
That hail thee now from many a burnish'd deck,
And all-impatient wish to haste thy speed,
Shall never see thee reach yon western wave,
Shall never more salute thy rising beam.
How great and how sublime! to view afar
The floating navies cut the briny tide,
That seem two ancient forests dark'ning there.
As when on land the gather'd soldiers hear
Their Captain's word, they carefully obey,
Anon they open, and again they close,
Now form the column, or compleat the square,
As tho'one mind alone inform'd the whole.
E'en so the tow'ring ships, with agile course,
And ready motion bend a thousand ways,
With one accord, in swift variety.
Lords of the wind, that raging, yet obeys,
And fills their bosom'd sails, behold they form
The long-drawn lines, which near, and nearer come.
While unfurl'd ensigns streaming in the gale,
And cannon's brazen voice provoke the fight.
So oft when summer burns the fallow plain,
The rising South-wind meets th'opposing North,

Due negre nubi: ftrifciano ful fofco
Sen lifte ferpeggianti di fugace
Lume che nato muore, e ognor rinafce:
E in cupo minaccevole mugito
Suonan da lungi pregne l'ampio grembo
Di ruinofa grandine, le guata
Lo fmarrito bifolco, al chiufo ovile
La fparfa greggia affretta, e il timorofo
Sguardo alla bionda meffe, alle crefcenti
Uve rivolge pallido, e fofpira.
Vedete là dove più irato tuona
Marte in feral rimbombo, ove la denfa
Caligine guerriera è rotta appena
Dalla fulminea luce, che lampeggia
Fra i cavi bronzi, in formidabil fronte
L'Anglo Duce apparir? vedete come
Son fifi in lui tutti gli fguardi? udite
Suonar ful labbro fuo voci prefaghe
Di ruina, e d'orror, voci che il Fato
Tacito approva, e che le negre fuore
Colle forfici aperte odono attente?
A di lui cenni, che ripeton l'aure
Sulle agitate infegne, i fuoi feroci
Compagni impazìenti in più riftretta
Pugna fcaglianfi a un tempo, come al cenno
Del negro Re per le difchiufe porte

In conflict fierce, and in aerial space
The angry Heavens roll forth their sable clouds
That crash together, forked lightnings dart
Their momentary rage, repeated still,
While awful thunder rolls the peal around,
And the sharp hail descends with ruinous force.
Scared at the storm, the shepherd drives his flock
To some near covert, and with sorr'wing eye
With visage pale, and bosom heaving deep,
Views his rich harvests, and his ripening vines.
Hark to the thunder of the God of war!
See how the smoky volumes curl on high,
Which lightnings darted forth from hollow guns
Can scarcely pierce, yonder the English chief,
With threat'ning eye, and dauntless front appears:
Observe on him is fix'd the gen'ral gaze,
While from his lips roll forth the accents dire,
Presaging wide destruction, and despair.
Lo silent Destiny attentive smiles,
And the dark sisters ope the fatal shears.
At his command, which the swift air repeats,
With many a streaming flag, the warriors rush
Fierce, and impatient, on the daring foe
In closer combat; so the sweeping winds
Burst from the cavern'd rocks, and mountains drear,
Forced by the sable monarch's stern decree.

Con fremito confufo efcono i venti.

Di faggio Duce, e di guerriero ardito
Adempier fa le parti, ei coll'efempio
Comanda, e i cenni fuoi fegue, chi fegue
Le tracce fue: dov'è il maggior periglio
Tutti ei precorre: in vano il franco Duce
Di mobil rocca alta ed immenfa mole
Gli muove incontro, e d'altre infiem riftrette
Fulminee frore folto argin guerriero
Gl'oppone: ei l'urta, apre, sbaraglia, e paffa
Rapido innanzi, qual fralle crefcenti
Tenere piante il turbine veftito
Di negre nubi che fulle fonanti
Ali di fuoco la tempefta porta.
Già la pugna ei mefce, e ad effa in mezzo
Come nel regno fuo fpazia la morte,
Che colla falce egual miete indiftinte
Le tefte illuftri, e le plebee, trafitti
Già cadon i più prodi, e d'un caduto
Quafi incontro al trionfo e non a morte
Mille corrono al pofto, ed a vicenda
Cadono anch'effi, vola a loro innanzi
La Fama, e in una man regge la tromba
Che l'uom trae dal fepolcro e in vita il ferba,
Agita l'altra un rilucente fpeglio,
Ove il guerriero che s'affifa è cieco

And now th'immortal leader, wife, and brave,
Commands, and gives th'example, thofe obey
The beft, who follow where his valour leads,
Still foremoft where fevereft dangers rife.
In vain the Gallic Admiral directs
His boyant fortrefs to oppofe the rage,
And pours his num'rous veffel's thunder forth;
The warlike Briton breaks the baffled line,
That all difperfed in hafty tumult flies.
So the wild wirlwind tears the tender trees,
When on thick clouds the winged horrour fails.
Now the fight rages, and amidft the fcene,
His own dire Empire, ftalks triumphant. death;
And with impartial fcythe, alike deftroys
Th'illuftrious Heroes, and the vulgar brave.
Firft the moft valiant fall, and ftill they come
A quick fucceffion, all in turn to die.
They feem to hafte to triumph, not to fate,
Fame flies before them, and in one hand bears
Her facred trump, that from the filent tomb
Can call the warriors to eternal life;
The other hand a burnish'd Mirrour shows,

E

A ogni mortal periglio: ognor s'accrefce
L'orror, la crudeltà, la tema, il lutto.
Delle fublimi torreggianti prore
Squarcianfi i duri fianchi, ove con rauco
Sibilante ftridor s'apron la ftrada
Fulminei globi: fendonfi fdrucite
Cigolando le vele, e di pendente
Ciurma ripieni con terribil fcoppio
Cadono, come fe dal folgor tronchi
Gl'arbori, e ftampan full'amico piano
Di membra infrante cruda orma di morte.
Fifchian le rotte fcheggie, e volan mifte
Alle recife membra, e pe'fumofi
Aerei campi di fanguigni fpruzzi
Traggon terribil traccia; rubicondi
Rivi di morte grondan fu i fpalmati
Neri fianchi, a cui intorno il flutto ondeggia
Atro di rofie fpume i femivivi
Cadaveri ingoiando. Oh qual ftupenda
Scena d'orrore! intanto i rauchi ftridi
Di chi chiede mercè, di chi fi muore
Il flebil mormorio, di chi s'adira
Le grida minacciofe, gl'ululati
Del vincitor del vinto infiem confufi
Col tuon guerrier, col fibilo del vento
Col fremito del mar l'orecchie introna

Wherein the brave who caſt an ardent eye,
Are blind to each encreaſing danger round;
Horrour, and ſavage rage, and bitter groans.
The mighty veſſels daſh their vengeful ſides
Against each other like oppoſing tow'rs,
While rapid globes a fiery paſſage force.
Rent are the uſeleſs ſails, and many a maſt,
High peopled with a pendant crowd, the ſhock
Brings headlong down, and on the purple floor,
With shatter'd limbs imprints the ſtamp of death.
The broken ſplinters ſend a dreadful ſound
Midſt the torn members, in the deep of air,
As thro' the ſmoke they mark a courſe of blood.
Now crimſon rivers waſh the ſable ſides
Of the proud ships, while round the foamy waves
Diſtain'd with gore, involve the quiv'ring dead.
O ſcene of Horrour! here are heard the cries
Of ſuppliant pity, here are dying groans,
There are loud ſhouts of Vict'ry, and Deſpair,
Mingled with brazen thunder, the mad winds
Howl terrible, and labouring Ocean roars.

D'atro rimbombo, e forma un indiftinto
Afpro concento, orribile armonìa.

O fpaventevol fuon ! voce fatale
Di Bellona e di Marte, che de'vili
Piombi ful cor con paurofo gelo,
Tu fei fprone al valore; e qual fovente
Dal curvo vetro ftropicciato, e volto
In giri rapidiffimi, fi parte
Vapor, che di celefte arcano fuoco
Empie le membra sì che cento, e cento
Vibran per ogni lato ignei zampilli;
Tal del nobil Garzon l'intrepid'alma
Viepiù s'infiamma al fero fuon di Marte,
E nel vivace afpetto e negl'ardenti
Occhi và fcintillando il generofo
Fuoco che il cor de'Patriotti accende.
Già più non cape in fe, già non gli fembra
Pofto onorato affai fe non là dove
E' il periglio più grande, il legno ardito
Spinge in mezzo a i nemici, e qual con fpeffi
Colpi iterati in ful ruftico tetto
Talor l'eftiva grandine rifuona,
Così ful legno cadono frequenti
I fulmini guerrieri, ei più s'avanza
Per vie di morte: fanguinofo e rotto
Gli cade innanzi il Giglio, o dal fuo legno

Confufion wild, and Harmony fevere.

O tumult dire! Bellona's fatal voice,

The voice of Mars, now makes the timid fhrink

With gelid fear, but fpurs the valiant on.

As when th' electric' globe in rapid round

Is turn'd, a flame myfterious fparkles forth,

And fills th' approaching limbs with wond'rous fire,

So the young Hero's gen'rous foul grows hot

While horrour thickens, rage inflames his cheek,

And patriot valour flashes from his eye.

Now too, infpired beyond himfelf, he finds

Where'er he goes a dearth of living fame,

Except where direft dangers threaten round.

He fteers his daring veffel midft the foe,

While warlike lightnings pierce it's riven fides,

Like sharp hail patt'ring on the ruftic roof.

Onward he moves thro' many a lane of death,

While the torn lily bleeding, at the view

Fra maraviglia, e fra terror s'arretra.
Intanto ful fatal campo di Marte
Fin dall'Elifie fedi il vol fpiegaro
Gl'Eroi Britanni. Primo in regio manto
Sotto di cui fplende l'usbergo e il brando,
Veniva d'Albion foftegno e Padre
Il grande Alfredo, che il tiranno giogo
Franfe del Dano, e in armi nere involto (*a*)

(*a*) Il famofo Principe di Galles figlio d'Eduardo III.
detto il Principe Nero dalla fopravefta delle fue armi. Egli ruppe i Francefi in due delle più celebri bat-
taglie, cioè in quella detta di *Creci* e nell'altra di *Po-
tiers*; avanti di dar quefta feconda trovavafi rinchiufo
con non più di 12 mila Inglefi da un efercito di circa
50 mila Francefi comandati dal Re fteffo in perfona;
in vece di renderfi con una vergognofa capitolazione
propoftagli, affalì coraggiofamente i nemici, gli fcon-
fiffe, e fece prigione lo fteffo Re. Quantunque ei foffe
nel fervore della giovinezza, quantunque irritato dal-
l'orgoglio de i nemici avanti la battaglia, moftrò dopo
la vittoria tutta la moderazione. Trattò colla più alta
reverenza il Re prigioniero, lo fervì a tavola, e ri-
cusò fempre rifpettofamente di federfi ivi con lui;
ma lo conduffe prigioniero a Londra. Quefto illuftre
Principe tanto degno del nome di Eroe non giunfe
mai a regnare, effendo morto immaturamente avanti
a fuo Padre. Hume Ift. d'Inghilt.

Droops her sad head, or all in terrour flies.
Now Albion's long-lost heroes, from the shades
  Of fair Elyfium, seek the martial scene.
  And first in royal robes, that proudly flow'd
  O'er the fierce falchion, and the coat of mail,
  Great Alfred came, father, and bulwark too
  Of ancient Britain, for his care of old
  Broke the tirannic Dane's imperious yoke,

Que' che di Gallia fopra il vinto fuolo
Corfe trionfatore, e con umile
Fronte d'un Re cattivo il fegue l'ombra:
E quei che diede alle Brittanne infegne (a)
Del Mar l'impero, e al Batavo feroce,
Per la novella libertate altiero,
Fiaccò l'orgoglio, di Signor tiranno
Servo fedele: e quei che fulle fponde
Del Danubio e del Ren tante difperfe
Nemiche fquadre, (b) e vacillar più volte
Fè fu gallica fronte il ferto Ibero:
E cento altre guerriere ombre la chioma
Cinte dell'immortal vittrice fronda
Pendean full'ali miniftrando forza
Spirando ardire entro a i Brittanni petti.
Riconobber con gioja i valorofi
Non degeneri Figli, e d'alto plaufo
Rimbombar fero armonico concento
In fuon più che mortal, che nella tromba
Della Fama raccolto ognor più echeggia,

(a) L'Ammiraglio Blake, che comandò le Flotte Inglefi nel tempo di Cromwel fpecialmente contro gli
Olandefi, fotto il qual Comandante la Marina Inglefe
cominciò a divenir la Sovrana del Mare.

(b) Il celebre Duca di Malborough.

And there the *fable Warrior*, § *mighty Prince!*
Who march'd triumphant o'er *fubjeffed France*,
Came haughty forth, while the majeftic shade
Of the once captive King his courfe attends.
And * He was there who gave the Britifh flag
Proud empire o'er the fea, and humbled low
The ftern Batavian, of new freedom vain;
A faithful fervant to a tyrant lord.
And † He, who routed oft the fquadron'd foe
Where the fwift Rhine, or Danube rolls the wave.
And shook on Gallic front th' Iberian crown.
A hundred other warlike shades were there,
Their locks with never-fading laurels bound,
And as they fail with outftrech'd wings, excite
Courage, and vigour, in the Britis'h hearts.
Full well they know their not degen'rate fons,
Full well their valour know, and from on high
Pour forth th' harmonious notes of loud applaufe,
With more than mortal voice, while fame repeats
The folemn found with thrilling trump a far.

---

§ *Edward the Black Prince.*
* *Admiral Blake.*
† *The famous Duke of Malborough.*

Suon che a profana orecchia mai non giunge,
E afcoltarlo talor folo è conceſſo
Ai Vati ed agl'·Eroi. Ma tu che in mezzo
Del venerabil coro, ombra guerriera
Del gran Roberto (a) fra cotanti fplendi
Trofei, perchè di duol nube funeſta ·
L'auguſto volto adombra, e una dolente,
Stilla mal trattenuta in· fù i pietoſi
Occhi s'affaccia? Ah già l'ora ferale
Vola con ali nere·intorno al Prode
Nipote, ah foſpendete il colpo o Numi,
E il fuo valore a·grandi opre ſerbate.
Ahi che priego mortal giammai non franſe
L'adamantina legge! apportatore
D'irreparabil danno ecco che fende
L'aria lo ſtrale; e il nobil fianco impiaga.
Il Giovinetto Eroe con fermo ciglio
Mira ſgorgar dalla mortal ferita
In larghi flutti il fangue, il piè vacilla,
E la Virtù più che la forza regge
Le membra inferme e male ubbidienti
All'intrepido ſpirto, e fe fi lagna
Si lagna fol della fcemata forza

_____

(a) Celebre Antenato Guerriero dell' Eroe del Poema.

Sound, never heard as yet by ear profane,
But granted only by indulgent Heaven,
To warm the Hero's, and the Poet's breast.
But thou brave * *Leader! who amidst the crowd*
Of Warriors so renown'd, distinguish'd stand'st.
And show'st thy well-earn'd trophies, say what grief
Hangs on thy solemn brow, why is that cheek
Bedew'd with falling tears? alas! pale death
O'er thy descendant broods with dark'ning wing.
Avert the coming stroke ye heavenly powers!
And save the youth for Virtue and his friends,
Nor let him perish by untimely stroke.
But vain are vows, and supplication vain,
To change the adamantine laws of fate;
For now O dreadful moment! thro' the air
The iron messenger of wrath, and woe,
Comes with relentless force, and rends the side
Of the ill-fated youth, with mortal wound.
With steady eye he views the gushing blood,
And only valour now sustains his frame.
Nor does he mourn, but that his valiant sword

---

* *Lord Robert Manners a celebrated Ancestor of the*
Hero of this Poem.

Al miglior uopo, e accufa il corpo frale
Il corpo difertor dell'alma invitta,
Frenate il fangue amici, ed il fugace
Spirto deh trattenete: ah che gl'eftremi
Momenti per gl'Eroi fono i più belli.
Nella fragil prigion fermati, e godi
Del tuo trionfo almeno: oh qual vendetta
Marte prepara a te! mira qual fulto
Stuol di nemiche vittime trafitte
Precede l'ombra tua! rimira, oh dolce
Anche a chi muor fpettacolo gradito!
Mira cadér rotto e sfiorato il giglio
Per ogni parte a te d'avanti: ofcura
Nube d'orror fi fparge or fra i difperfi
Già pompofi veffilli: altri lo fcampo
Alle rapide fida ali del vento,
Altri lo cerca invan: l'invitto Duce,
Che primo urtando de'nemici legni
Lo ftretto ordine aperfe, e di feguaci
Guerriere prore doppo fe traendo
Un lungo ftuol vi penetrò, qual fuole
Fiamma talor con luminofa ftrifcia
Correr fcoppiando per le bionde meffi,
La pieghevole fila or curva in ampio
Orrido cerchio, e le nemiche prore
Già fegnate dal Fato, e già fortite

Can never more defend his country's cauſe.
While his dim eye, in ſorrow ſeems t'accuſe
His body, ſinking from his vig'rous mind.
Ye his bold Comrades ſtop the crimſon tide!
Nor let his gen'rous ſoul eſcape to heaven!
But oh how glorious is his dying hour!
Yet hov'ring ſpirit one short moment pauſe!
To feel the transport to proud triumph due.
And mark the vengeance of terrific Mars,
What num'rous victims wait thy parting ſhade;
With raptur'd eye gaze on the ſplendid ſcene,
While low the Gallic lilies droop around,
And mid the fallen ſtandards, horrour frowns.
Now midſt the battle, ſome their ſafety find
On wings of rapid winds, and ſome in vain
Seek to eſcape; The chief invincible,
Firſt to oppoſe the foe, the long-drawn fleet
With vigour forces, breaks their order fair,
And with him brings unnumber'd vengeful ſails.
E'en ſo full oft, a lum'nous train of fire
Conſumes with ſpreading noiſe the yellow corn.
But now in dreadful bend his line proceeds,
And quick ſurrounds the wond'ring enemy,
And the proud ships, by deſtiny decreed

Per olocaufto, o per trofeo di Marte
Circonda e preme: in cupa notte involto
Il difordine cieco errando vola
Sulle racchiufe vele, e i vili e i forti
Mefce e fcompiglia : in mezzo al fumo, al fangue
Ordine più non v'è, nè più de Duci
S'odono i cenni, i mal fegnati colpi
Cadon fu i legni amici, e in preda all'onde
Or tratte ora refpinte urtanfi infieme
Ed antenne ad antenne e prore a prore:
Quai d'annofa forefta i pini i cerri,
Quando gli rota in polverofi giri
L'ala del turbin fero in rauco ftrido
Cozzan tronchi con tronchi, e le ramofe
Braccia fchiantate con fracaffo orrendo
Volteggiano per l'aere. Ancor refifte
Il Gallico valor: ma quando alfine
Rotto e fanguigno il tuo primier veffillo,
O Graffe fventurato, in umil atto
Supplice s'abbafsò: cade il coraggio
Manca all'alme il vigor le deftre ai colpi.
Ma voi che nol feguifte e l'onorata
Voftra caduta almeno in fugl'alati
Verfi porti la Fama e narri come
Vi fu l'onor più della vita caro: (a)

_____

(a) Si defcrive quì ciò che realmente avvenne, un
legno calato a fondo, ed uno bruciato.

To be the prize, the triumph of his pow'r.
Now blind confusion flies with erring wing
Midst the restricted vessels, and alike
Baffles the valiant, and confounds the base,
While thro' the bloody scene, and smoky clouds,
No order reigns, none bear their chiefs controul,
But friends with friends, in blindest rage contend.
Left to the mercy of th' indignant waves,
Against each other dash the careless prows,
And masts encounter masts, as shatter'd trees
Of some old forest, when the hurricane
Comes on with ruthless force; in conflict dire
Torn branches mingle, and opposing trunks
With horrid tumult sweep the plains of air.
The val'rous Gauls e'en still resist, but soon
As e'er thy leading flag, O sad De-Grasse!
Broken, and bloody, sinks it's humbled head,
Their courage sickens, and their force is o'er.
But O for you, brave warriors who escaped.
His shameful fate, the tuneful muse shall tell,
That you prefer'd your glory to your life.

Sparga di fior grata la Patria il voftro
Sepolcro, e quai fopra l'Eurota un giorno,
S'allegrin più del voftro ultimo fato
Che dello fcampo altrui Galliche Madri.
Nel circolo fatale onde di morte
Piove tuttora il grandinofo nembo
Stà il legno ardito, e quale Orfa che cinta
Da' Cacciatori, e che nel fianco fenta
Il duro fpiedo infuria, e il dente e l'unghia
Difpiegando s'avventa incontro all'armi:
Tal fquarciato in più lati, e ancor non vinto,
Nè invendicato, ancor refifte, e folo ·
La gloria cerca di cader da forte:
Ma ne laceri fianchi ampia fineftra
Apron ftridendo i replicati colpi
De' ferrei globi, da più lati in feno
Già mormorando in cupo fuon di morte
L'onda fatal vi paffa, ecco s'inchina
La proda, ecco s'immerge, il legno affonda;
Invan le palme i fupplici occhi e il volto
Stendono al Ciel le moribonde turbe,
E mentre invan co piedi e colle braccia
Vanfi avinghiando infiem, manca al lor piede
L'inftabil pavimento, il legno alfine
Sparifce, e in fpeffi e vorticofi giri
L'onda fpumando fopra lui fi chiude.

Yet still your Country shall all-grateful shed
Upon your tomb the od'rous pride of spring,
And as of old, on fair Eurota's banks,
The Gallic Mothers with delight prefer
Your glorious death, to safety unrenown'd.
His desp'rate vessel moves amidst the rage
Of fierce surrounding fate, as some wild bear
By hunters wounded, while the thirsty darts
Drink his hot blood, with fury opes his jaws,
And springs with rapid force upon the foe.
E'en so the ship, tho' shatter'd in the fight
Itself defends, tho' masts, and sails, are gone,
Yet still in yielding it appears to strive
To merit honour, and be lost with glory.
But iron balls from brazen cannon sent,
Force frequent openings in it's wounded sides,
And with terrific roar the whelming flood
Rushes impetuous in, while low the prow
Stoops in the bosom of the yawning deep,
Then in the fearful moment, the pale crowd
Lift up imploring hands, and eyes, to heaven,
In tender close embrace, each clings to each,
And so they sink, for ever, ever lost,
While smiling eddies dimple on the main.

F

Già da ogni parte prigioniero e vinto
Sparito è il Giglio: i trionfali gridi
Infra il fangue l'orror, fra le querele
De'moribondi, e de'languenti al Cielo
Ergon feftofi d'Albione i Figli.
Invan tregua han le ftragi, ancor fatolla
Non è l'ingorda morte; invan la notte
Sorge pietofa, e coll'opaco velo
Copre il fangue, le ftragi, infiem confonde
I vincitori i vinti, e fi frappone
Fra l'ire de'mortali: invan dell'armi
E' fofpefo il fragor: dal rauco fuono
Di difperate ftrida è rotto a un tratto
Il notturno filenzio, e il negro orrore
Fugato da improvvifo orrido lume,
Ch'efce dal fen d'un prigioniero legno,
Ove occulto s'apprefe, e ferpeggiando
Crebbe il fuoco in incendio, in fluttuanti
Spire le fiamme ergonfi in alto, il cupo
Ciel fi difcuopre, e le notturne nubi
Dipinte in roffo, il tenebrofo velo
Ritrae la notte dal ceruleo feno
De'luccicanti flutti, ove diftefe
E ripercoffe tremolanti ondeggiano
Dell'alto incendio le appuntate cime.

The valiant lily diſappears around,

   And Britain's ſhouting ſons, amid the ſcene

   Of groans, and death, the air loud-echoing rend.

   In vain the carnage ceaſes, vainly night

   With veil obſcure comes on to hide the view

   Of slaughter, and deſtruction, and confounds

   Alike the conquer'd, and the conquerors.

   Huſht is the voice of war, but huſht in vain,

   For midſt the ſilent hour, a dreadful ſound,

   Is heard to riſe, of deſolate deſpair:

   While a fierce blaze of light darts from the ſide

   Of one late captur'd ship, with horrid rage.

   In ſpiry volumes mount the vengeful flames,

   And darkneſs flies, while the ſurrounding clouds

   Are ſtreak'd with crimſon glow, and from the waves

   Now brightly blue, the ſable night is fled,

   While on the ſurge reflected fires are ſeen.

Fra il cupo orror fcoffo da incerti raggi
Di chiaro vacillante, in full'amica
Flotta, fra gl'albor rotti e le fquarciate
Sanguigne prore all'ampie fiamme in faccia
Cento attoniti vifi appaion tinti
Di roffeggiante luce: intanto il vento
L'incendio avviva, fulle ardenti vele
Rapido fcorre, le abbronzate funi
Schiantanfi, cadon giù mifte e confufe
Infiem l'aere avvampando antenne e gabbie,
Infelici guerrieri, e che vi valfe
Comprar la vita al caro e duro prezzo
Di vergognofa fervitù, fe Morte
Non fazia ancor le vittime richiede
Dall'ira fua fcampate? efce dal feno
Dell'incendio crudele il flebil grido
Della turba che muore, e fi confonde
Collo ftridor della vorace fiamma,
Che ognor s'abbaffa, ed il ceruleo dorfo
Già lambifce dell'onda, alfin penetra,
Dove fopito in neri grani giace
Il folgore di Marte, e appena tocco
Da piccola fcintilla ecco lampeggia
Quafi baleno, e con orrendo fcoppio
Spezza e fracaffa dell'ardente legno
Le fumanti reliquie: alzanfi a volo

Thro' the thick gloom pierc'd by the trembling light,
Behold the British fleet, while mid the mafts,
And shatter'd prows, appear in wild amaze
A thoufand faces tinged with flaming red.
By the ftrong wind excited, the fwift fire
Confumes the fails, and cords, with ardent rage,
While the mafts tumble from their airy height.
O wretched Warriors! little now avails,
T'have purchafed life by bafe captivity,
Since death infatiate claims you for his own,
Sad victims! who had hoped t'efcape his pow'r!
Now from the furious blaze, a mingled cry
Is heard of deep defpair; mid the wild roar
Of quick-devouring flames, that foon defcend
To the blue bofom of th'affrighted deep.
At length the burning fury penetrates
Where the dark powder all collected lies;
The cannons vigour, and the nerve of war.
Soon as a fpark here enter'd, thro' the air
With dire explofion, and the light'nings fpeed,
The fmoky ruin rufhes to the fky,

In ampi giri i fcintillanti tronchi,
E a mille a mille l'infocate fcheggie,
E della notte il tenebrofo feno
Segnan cadendo con fiammanti ftrifce.
Così dall' Adriana eccelfa mole
Sul biondo Tebro ed i romani tetti
Tra il frequente fcoppiar delle vibrate
Sulfuree canne, e tra feftofi gridi
Luminofa talor pioggia fi verfa.
Fugge la notte omai ful biancheggiante
Carro a i rofei corfier fcotendo il freno
L' Alba rifveglia la natura, e fcopre
Le ruine di Marte, e tutti i danni
Del fanguinofo dì, della vittoria
L' ardor, la cieca ebrietà fi fcioglie
In penfierofa calma: or mira quanto
Sangue a lui cofti il vincitore ifteffo
La palma combattuta. Ombre onorate
Che d' Albìon fulle dilette fpiagge
Forfe ancor v' aggirate, il fo, contente
Siete di voftra forte: è troppo bello
Morir così, ma fia che a ciglio afciutto
Miri la Patria il voftro eftremo fato?
Ah sì lo miri, e con un mifto affetto
Di riverenza e di ftupor trattenga

And scatters many a blazing fragment round,
Tinging the night obscure with lucid glow.
E'en so is seen from Adrian's lofty fane
On festal day the fiery shower descend,
And gild the structures near, and brightly shine
In yellow Tyber's wave, midst clam'rous shouts.
Dun Night retires, and bright Aurora comes
In silver car, with reins of roseate hue
She guides her eager coursers, nature feels
Her lov'd approach, while the clear ray displays
Horrid disasters, and the bloody scene
Of Mars, who triumph'd the preceding day.
Now the blind rage of conquest, valour too
Subside in pensive transitory calm;
And the proud victors see what streams of blood
Were pour'd, ere they obtain'd the palm renown'd.
Ye honour'd shades! who still perhaps delight
To haunt lov'd Albion's shores, and are content
Thus to have died, for sweet is death like yours.
Say shall your Country thinking on your fate,
Refuse to sadly shed the heart-felt tear?
Ah yes! for she beholds you, and restrains
The liquid grief, while wonder most profound,
And awful rev'rence all her thoughts subdue.

Il duolo intempeſtivo, e ſulle voſtre
Belle ferite prezìoſi pegni
Di virtù di valor fiſi lo ſguardo
Tacito immoto, e altro dal ciel non chieda
Che Figli a voi ſimili : ma qual alma
V'à coſì dura, che ſu tuoi freſch'anni
Giunti ſì toſto a ſera in ſul comune
Danno non ſparga un ſoſpir tronco almeno
Prode Roberto? a te che giova intorno
Veder ſoſpeſi i trionfali allori,
E le nemiche prigioniere inſegne
Compre col ſangue tuo? della vittoria
A te che giova i plauſi udir? ſe rotto
Lo ſtame tuo vital più non ſoſtenta
L'anima grande la languente ſalma.
L'atro pallor di morte diſcolora
La roſea faccia già dal ſacro fuoco
Di Marte tinta: l'infallibil dardo
Scocca, tranquillo e fermo egli l'attende
Con quella calma placida, ch'è figlia
Della Virtù: pochi momenti ancora
Gli concede il deſtino, egli co'lumi
Già dal velo di morte ingombri mira
Le ſue belle ferite, e mentre gode
In penſar quanto glorìoſo e dolce
E' il morir per la Patria, il gelo eſtremo

Her *ſtedfaſt eye upon your gaping wounds*
In *ſorrow fixes, wounds, that valour prove;*
Then *asks from Heaven for other ſons like you.*
But *who can think of your too tranſient life*
Nor *heave one ſtruggling ſigh for Britain's loſs.*
What *boots it you that captive colours wave,*
And *laurels flouriſh which your blood obtain'd,*
What *boots it you that Vict'ry ſhouts aloud,*
And *ſoaring fame her trump wide-echoing ſounds,*
Since *low alas! your valiant limbs are laid!*
Pale *is that face where late the flame of war*
Mix'd *it's bright luſtre with benignant looks.*
From *fatal bow the ruthleſs dart of death*
Sprung *rapidly, while Manners void of fear*
Th' *approaching moment ſaw, and all reſign'd*
Met *his ſad fate, with firmneſs, only known*
To *gen'rous Virtue, and her moſt-loved ſons.*
Careleſs *he view'd his wounds, and thought the while*
How *ſweet it was to die in Britain's cauſe.*

Gl'irrigidifce a poco a poco i membri,
E nel mortal fopor cade e vien meno
Con quel foave oblio con quella pace,
Con cui talor s'adagia, e i lumi chiude
Innocente fanciullo in dolce fonno.
Trattieni, o Mufa, del dolente plettro
L'imbelle fuono, e con lugubri note
D'un Eroe non offender la grand'ombra.
Voi chiamo in teftimoni, anime invitte,
Che all'aura trionfal di libertade
Fofte nutrite, e un cuor ferbate in feno
Degno d'un tanto dono, e chi può mai
Senza invidia mirar morte sì bella?
Chi non vorrebbe a i brevi giorni illuftri
Di quefto Eroe pofporre inglorìofa
Neftorea etade? o forfennati, o ciechi
Mortali che con fubito tremore
Raccapricciando ritorcete indietro
L'occhio e il penfier fuggendo dalla nera
Vana larva di morte che v'inganna
,, Come falfo veder beftia quand'ombra!
Sapete voi perchè natura fparfe
Tanto orror ful fin noftro, e di sì fcure
Tenebre fpaventofe lo coperfe?
Per ritenerci in vita, ed impedirci
Di difertar dal dolorofo pofto,

Then the last frost seized on his clay-cold corse,

And wrapt the Hero in oblivious rest;

So the soft Infant calmly sinks to sleep.

But cease O Muse! th' unwarlike harp to sound

With plaintive notes, that but displease his shade.

O say unconquer'd souls! who long have dwelt

Beneath the sunshine of fair liberty,

And who deserve the ray, say can you see

Unenvied his proud fate, nor yet desire

In the same glorious track to shed your blood.

Who would not rather share the early fate

Of this brave youth, than live thro Nestor's years,

Unnoticed, unesteem'd, in useless ease.

O senseless Mortals! who with fearful eye

Gaze on the melancholy spectre, Death,

But spectre vain; which sadly cheats our sight

As the false shade some roving beast alarms:

Know that wise Nature spreads a horrid veil,

And thickest darkness o'er the end of life,

In cui ci mife fra miferie e ftenti;
E chi fenza il fatale e cupo foffo
Che fta di vita in ful confine ofcuro,
E ci fpaventa al falto, e chi potrebbe
Soffrire o il duol dell' egre membra, o i danni
Dell' imbecille età cadente, o i morfi
D' amor, di gelosìa, de' fcellerati
Potenti il duro ed infultante orgoglio,
Degl' amici infedeli i tradimenti,
La rabbia de' Tiranni? Oh morte orrendo
Fantafma ai vili! oh defiato punto,
,, Che l' umana miferia fuol far breve
A i forti! oh di qual nuova luce adorna
Tu fei quando apparifci al prode al faggio
Quafi a far plaufo, e delle fue bell' opre
La fine a coronar: perchè fu quefto
Mar procellofo della vita, mentre
Naviga incerto in mezzo agl' inquìeti
Affetti, e come mai vivrà ficuro
Di non macchiar dell' onorate imprefe
Fino all' ultimo dì la nobil tela?
Salve o facro momento, in cui la Fama
Segna i volumi fuoi del gloriofo
Indelebil figillo: io ti rimiro
Volar con brune ma foavi penne
Sul mio giovine Eroe, come gentile

Lest by desertion we should fly our woes.
And had she not on life's dread bound'ry placed
An awful gulph, in mists obscurely hid,
To check the wretch's leap from human cares;
None, none would bear the deeply-rending pains
Of fell disease, or sad declining age,
Love's wildest pangs, or Jealousy's despair,
" The insolence of Office, or the spurns
That patient merit from th' unworthy takes, "
The treach'rous Friend, and bloody tyrant's rage.
O Death by cowards dreaded, by the brave
Desired, dear moment that subdues our woes!
Thou'rt grateful to the valiant, and the wise,
The meed of all their actions, and the crown.
For He who sails on life's tempestuous Sea,
Can ne'er be certain of unalter'd glory.
Hail sacred moment when recording fame
Stamps on her awful page th' eternal seal.

Aura che forta dopo burafcofa
Guerra d' Auftro e di Noto il vacillante
Sdrucito legno alfin conduce in porto.
Intanto là nel gelido foggiorno,
  Dove tra ricchi iftoriati marmi
  Morte fiede pompofa, io t' accompagno
O nobil falma: in quefto muto albergo,
Ove la Patria accoglie de'più degni
Figli la fredda fpoglia, in fra le fculte
Pietre che lacrimando erge ella fteffa (a),
Fra i Guerrieri, fra i Re, fra i Saggi, in mezzo
A ftuol sì illuftre placida ripofa.
Verranno a te quafi di Marte all'ara
Le genti d' Albion: le vaghe Figlie
Atteggiate di doglia e di pietade
Verferan di dolor leggiadre ftille:
Lacrime di piacer ful freddo faffo
Verferà la vecchiezza in te mirando
Che l' Anglico valor non è ancor fpento:
Dolce pianto d' invidia i tuoi guerrieri
Compagni, e innanzi a te con eloquente
Maeftofo filenzio in quella immerfi

(a) Per decreto del parlamento è ftato fabbricato
il Sepolcro a Lord Manners nell'Abbazia di Weft-
minfter, ove fon pofte le tombe degl'uomini i più
rifpettabili d'Inghilterra.

I view her hover o'er the val'rous youth,
With dark, but gentle pinion, so full oft
Mild breezes, when the troub'lous war is o'er
Twixt the sharp East wind, and the roaring West,
Impell the shatter'd veffel into port.
But I, O Noble Corfe! will follow thee
Where lordly Death, in defolate abode
Of rich, and floried Marble, filent fits.
In this mute refidence, illuftrious Shade!
Repofe at peace! for here your Country calls
Her beft-lov'd fons, which are her worthieft too,
Midft fculptured monuments herfelf has rais'd;
Kings, fcholars, warriors, here together fleep.
The generous Britons croud around his tomb,
As 'twere the shrine of Mars, and virgins fair,
Their lovely cheeks tinged by fad forrow's glow,
With many a pitying tear bedew the ftone.
And penfive age a doleful pleafure feels,
To find that British Valour is not fled.
Your lov'd Companions heave the emulous figh,
And view the facred fpot with ftedfaft gaze,
In filence wrapt, and thoughtful melancholy.

Eſtaſi ſacra degl'Eroi, la tomba
Contempleran con fermo immobil ciglio.
E mentre la grand'ombra errando ſopra
Le cerulee campagne, alle Britanne
Inſegne intorno a cuſtodir l'impero
Veglia del mare, e ſparge alto ſpavento
In fra i nemici ſuoi: la ſacra viſta
Di queſto marmo iſpirerà coraggio,
E di patrio valor ſtimoli ardenti
Ne' giovinetti Eroi, che a lui davanti
Sentian palpitar da i dolci moti
D'un emola virtù gl'anche ineſperti
Teneri cor; ſolleverà dall'imo
Suol ſpirando magnanimi penſieri
Ogn'alma patriottica, e con grande
Eſempio moſtrerà come ſi vive
Per la Patria, e per lei come ſi muore.

And while his facred Manes roams the sky,

Or loves to hover round the British flags,

Watchful to guard the empire of the fea,

And ftrike difmay, and anguish on the foe;

This hallow'd marble shall infpire the brave,

And in each tender, unexperienced mind,

Excite the gen'rous, patriotic flame:

Shall raife the foul to deeds of high renown,

And give a great example to mankind,

How for their country they should live, and die.

R. M.